How the Leopard Got His Spots and Other Just So Stories

RUDYARD KIPLING

Illustrated by Thea Kliros

DOVER PUBLICATIONS, INC.
New York

DOVER CHILDREN'S THRIFT CLASSICS
EDITOR: PHILIP SMITH

Published in Canada by General Publishing Company, Ltd., 30 Lesmill Road, Don Mills, Toronto, Ontario.

How the Leopard Got His Spots and Other Just So Stories is a new selection of six stories from *Just So Stories for Little Children,* first published by Doubleday, Page & Company, New York, 1902. The stories are printed here unabridged; however, the author's original illustrations (and illustration captions) have been replaced with new illustrations by Thea Kliros. A new introductory Note has also been specially prepared for this edition.

Manufactured in the United States of America
Dover Publications, Inc., 31 East 2nd Street, Mineola, N.Y. 11501

Library of Congress Cataloging-in-Publication Data

Kipling, Rudyard, 1865–1936.
    [Just so stories. Selections]
    How the leopard got his spots and other Just so stories / Rudyard Kipling ; illustrated by Thea Kliros.
        p.   cm. — (Dover children's thrift classics)
    Contents: How the whale got his throat — How the rhinoceros got his skin — How the leopard got his spots — The crab that played with the sea — The cat that walked by himself — The butterfly that stamped.
    ISBN 0-486-27297-4 (pbk.)
    1. Children's stories, English. [1. Animals—Fiction. 2. Short stories.] I. Kliros, Thea, ill. II. Title. III. Series.
PZ7.K632Hl   1992
[Fic]—dc20
                                        92-20780
                                         CIP
                                       AC

Note

An author equally celebrated for his children's as well as adult-oriented works, the English novelist, short story writer and poet Rudyard Kipling (1865–1936) enjoyed both critical praise and enormous public popularity during his lifetime. *Just So Stories*, along with the *Jungle Books*, *Kim* and *Captains Courageous*, has long been acclaimed as one of the essential works of the children's canon.

In this work, as in many of his other efforts, Kipling drew upon his experiences as a child and as a young man in British-ruled India. The *Just So Stories*, which grew out of tales spun orally for Kipling's children, combine the exoticism of the Raj with the author's playful and poetic language, creating ironic myths in which animals interact with people, and improbable accounts are given of the origins of their forms and ways.

The modern reader should be aware that Kipling's writings are of their times, and reflect the prevailing racial attitudes of white Europeans during the colonial era. Thus occasional passages containing offensive racial references have been retained as intrinsic to the author's cultural perspective.

Contents

List of Illustrations

How the Whale
Got His Throat

IN THE SEA, once upon a time, O my Best
Beloved, there was a Whale, and he ate
fishes. He ate the starfish and the garfish, and
the crab and the dab, and the plaice and the
dace, and the skate and his mate, and the
mackereel and the pickereel, and the really
truly twirly-whirly eel. All the fishes he could
find in all the sea he ate with his mouth—so!
Till at last there was only one small fish left in
all the sea, and he was a small 'Stute Fish, and
he swam a little behind the Whale's right ear,
so as to be out of harm's way. Then the Whale
stood up on his tail and said, 'I'm hungry.' And
the small 'Stute Fish said in a small 'stute
voice, 'Noble and generous Cetacean, have
you ever tasted Man?'

'No,' said the Whale. 'What is it like?'

'Nice,' said the small 'Stute Fish. 'Nice but
nubbly.'

1

'Then fetch me some,' said the Whale, and he made the sea froth up with his tail.

'One at a time is enough,' said the 'Stute Fish. 'If you swim to latitude Fifty North, longitude Forty West (that is Magic), you will find, sitting *on* a raft, *in* the middle of the sea, with nothing on but a pair of blue canvas breeches, a pair of suspenders (you must *not* forget the suspenders, Best Beloved), and a jack-knife, one shipwrecked Mariner, who, it is only fair to tell you, is a man of infinite-resource-and-sagacity.'

So the Whale swam and swam to latitude Fifty North, longitude Forty West, as fast as he could swim, and *on* a raft, *in* the middle of the sea, *with* nothing to wear except a pair of blue canvas breeches, a pair of suspenders (you must particularly remember the suspenders, Best Beloved), *and* a jack-knife, he found one single, solitary shipwrecked Mariner, trailing his toes in the water. (He had his Mummy's leave to paddle, or else he would never have done it, because he was a man of infinite-resource-and-sagacity.)

Then the Whale opened his mouth back and back and back till it nearly touched his tail, and he swallowed the shipwrecked Mariner, and the raft he was sitting on, and his blue canvas breeches, and the suspenders (which you *must* not forget), *and* the jack-knife—He swallowed them all down into his warm, dark, inside cupboards, and then he smacked his lips—so, and turned round three times on his tail.

But as soon as the Mariner, who was a man of infinite-resource-and-sagacity, found himself truly inside the Whale's warm, dark, inside cupboards, he stumped and he jumped and he thumped and he bumped, and he pranced and he danced, and he banged and he clanged, and he hit and he bit, and he leaped and he creeped, and he prowled and he howled, and he hopped and he dropped, and he cried and he sighed, and he crawled and he bawled, and he stepped and he lepped, and he danced hornpipes where he shouldn't, and the Whale felt most unhappy indeed. (*Have* you forgotten the suspenders?)

So he said to the 'Stute Fish, 'This man is very nubbly, and besides he is making me hiccough. What shall I do?'

'Tell him to come out,' said the 'Stute Fish.

So the Whale called down his own throat to the shipwrecked Mariner, 'Come out and behave yourself. I've got the hiccoughs.'

'Nay, nay!' said the Mariner. 'Not so, but far

He stumped and he jumped and he thumped and
he bumped.

otherwise. Take me to my natal-shore and the white-cliffs-of-Albion, and I'll think about it.' And he began to dance more than ever.

'You had better take him home,' said the 'Stute Fish to the Whale. 'I ought to have warned you that he is a man of infinite-resource-and-sagacity.'

So the Whale swam and swam and swam, with both flippers and his tail, as hard as he could for the hiccoughs; and at last he saw the Mariner's natal-shore and the white-cliffs-of-Albion, and he rushed half-way up the beach, and opened his mouth wide and wide and wide, and said, 'Change here for Winchester, Ashuelot, Nashua, Keene, and stations on the *Fitch*burg Road'; and just as he said 'Fitch' the Mariner walked out of his mouth. But while the Whale had been swimming, the Mariner, who was indeed a person of infinite-resource-and-sagacity, had taken his jack-knife and cut up the raft into a little square grating all running criss-cross, and he had tied it firm with his suspenders (*now* you know why you were not to forget the suspenders!), and he dragged that grating good and tight into the Whale's throat, and there it stuck! Then he recited the following *Sloka*, which, as you have not heard it, I will now proceed to relate—

> By means of a grating
> I have stopped your ating.

For the Mariner he was also an Hi-ber-ni-an. And he stepped out on the shingle, and went home to his Mother, who had given him leave to trail his toes in the water; and he married and lived happily ever afterward. So did the Whale. But from that day on, the grating in his throat, which he could neither cough up nor swallow down, prevented him eating anything except very, very small fish; and that is the reason why whales nowadays never eat men or boys or little girls.

The small 'Stute Fish went and hid himself in the mud under the Door-sills of the Equator. He was afraid that the Whale might be angry with him.

The Sailor took the jack-knife home. He was wearing the blue canvas breeches when he walked out on the shingle. The suspenders were left behind, you see, to tie the grating with; and that is the end of *that* tale.

WHEN the cabin port-holes are dark and green
 Because of the seas outside;
When the ship goes *wop* (with a wiggle between)
And the steward falls into the soup-tureen,
 And the trunks begin to slide;
When Nursey lies on the floor in a heap,
And Mummy tells you to let her sleep,
And you aren't waked or washed or dressed,
Why, then you will know (if you haven't guessed)
You're 'Fifty North and Forty West!'

How the Rhinoceros
Got His Skin

ONCE UPON A TIME, on an uninhabited island on the shores of the Red Sea, there lived a Parsee from whose hat the rays of the sun were reflected in more-than-oriental splendour. And the Parsee lived by the Red Sea with nothing but his hat and his knife and a cooking-stove of the kind that you must particularly never touch. And one day he took flour and water and currants and plums and sugar and things, and made himself one cake which was two feet across and three feet thick. It was indeed a Superior Comestible (*that's* Magic), and he put it on the stove because *he* was allowed to cook on that stove, and he baked it and he baked it till it was all done brown and smelt most sentimental. But just as he was going to eat it there came down to the beach from the Altogether Uninhabited Interior one Rhinoceros with a horn on his nose, two piggy eyes, and few manners. In those days the Rhinoceros's skin fitted him quite tight. There were no wrinkles in it anywhere. He looked exactly like a Noah's Ark Rhinoceros, but of course much bigger. All the same, he had no manners then, and he has no manners now, and he never will have any manners. He said, 'How!' and the Parsee left that cake and climbed to the top of a palm-tree with nothing on but his hat, from which the rays of the sun were always reflected in more-than-oriental splendour. And the Rhinoceros upset the oil-stove with his nose, and the cake rolled on the sand, and he spiked that cake on the horn of his nose, and he ate it, and he went away, waving his tail, to the desolate and Exclusively Uninhabited Interior which abuts on the islands of Mazanderan, Socotra, and the Promontories of the Larger Equinox. Then the Parsee came down from his palm-tree and put the stove on its legs and recited the following *Sloka*, which, as you have not heard, I will now proceed to relate:—

> Them that takes cakes
> Which the Parsee-man bakes
> Makes dreadful mistakes.

And there was a great deal more in that than you would think.

The Parsee left that cake and climbed to the top
of a palm-tree.

Because, five weeks later, there was a heat-
wave in the Red Sea, and everybody took off
all the clothes they had. The Parsee took off
his hat; but the Rhinoceros took off his skin
and carried it over his shoulder as he came
down to the beach to bathe. In those days it
buttoned underneath with three buttons and
looked like a waterproof. He said nothing
whatever about the Parsee's cake, because he
had eaten it all; and he never had any manners, then, since, or henceforward. He wad-
dled straight into the water and blew bubbles
through his nose, leaving his skin on the
beach.

Presently the Parsee came by and found the
skin, and he smiled one smile that ran all
round his face two times. Then he danced
three times round the skin and rubbed his
hands. Then he went to his camp and filled his
hat with cake-crumbs, for the Parsee never
ate anything but cake, and never swept out
his camp. He took that skin, and he shook
that skin, and he scrubbed that skin, and he
rubbed that skin just as full of old, dry, stale
tickly cake-crumbs and some burned currants
as ever it could *possibly* hold. Then he
climbed to the top of his palm-tree and waited
for the Rhinoceros to come out of the water
and put it on.

And the Rhinoceros did. He buttoned it up with the three buttons, and it tickled like cake-crumbs in bed. Then he wanted to scratch, but that made it worse; and then he lay down on the sands and rolled and rolled and rolled, and every time he rolled the cake-crumbs tickled him worse and worse and worse. Then he ran to the palm-tree and rubbed and rubbed and rubbed himself against it. He rubbed so much and so hard that he rubbed his skin into a great fold over his shoulders, and another fold underneath, where the buttons used to be (but he rubbed the buttons off), and he rubbed some more folds over his legs. And it spoiled his temper, but it didn't make the least difference to the cake-crumbs. They were inside his skin and they tickled. So he went home, very angry indeed and horribly scratchy; and from that day to this every rhinoceros has great folds in his skin and a very bad temper, all on account of the cake-crumbs inside.

But the Parsee came down from his palm-tree, wearing his hat, from which the rays of the sun were reflected in more-than-oriental splendour, packed up his cooking-stove, and went away in the direction of Orotavo, Amygdala, the Upland Meadows of Anan-tarivo, and the Marshes of Sonaput.

THIS Uninhabited Island
          Is off Cape Gardafui,
By the Beaches of Socotra
          And the Pink Arabian Sea:
But it's hot—too hot from Suez
          For the likes of you and me
                    Ever to go
                    In a P. and O.
          And call on the Cake-Parsee!

How the Leopard
Got His Spots

IN THE DAYS when everybody started fair,
Best Beloved, the Leopard lived in a place
called the High Veldt. 'Member it wasn't the
Low Veldt, or the Bush Veldt, or the Sour
Veldt, but the 'sclusively bare, hot, shiny High
Veldt, where there was sand and sandy-
coloured rock and 'sclusively tufts of sandy-
yellowish grass. The Giraffe and the Zebra
and the Eland and the Koodoo and the Harte-
beest lived there; and they were 'sclusively
sandy-yellow-brownish all over; but the Leopard, he was the 'sclusivest sandiest-yellow-
est-brownest of them all—a greyish-yellowish
catty-shaped kind of beast, and he matched
the 'sclusively yellowish-greyish-brownish
colour of the High Veldt to one hair. This was
very bad for the Giraffe and the Zebra and the
rest of them; for he would lie down by a 'sclusively yellowish-greyish-brownish stone or

clump of grass, and when the Giraffe or the
Zebra or the Eland or the Koodoo or the
Bush-Buck or the Bonte-Buck came by he
would surprise them out of their jumpsome
lives. He would indeed! And, also, there was
an Ethiopian with bows and arrows (a 'sclusively greyish-brownish-yellowish man he was
then), who lived on the High Veldt with the
Leopard; and the two used to hunt together—
the Ethiopian with his bows and arrows, and
the Leopard 'sclusively with his teeth and
claws—till the Giraffe and the Eland and the
Koodoo and the Quagga and all the rest of
them didn't know which way to jump, Best
Beloved. They didn't indeed!

After a long time—things lived for ever so
long in those days—they learned to avoid anything that looked like a Leopard or an Ethiopian; and bit by bit—the Giraffe began it,
because his legs were the longest—they went
away from the High Veldt. They scuttled for
days and days and days till they came to a
great forest, 'sclusively full of trees and
bushes and stripy, speckly, patchy-blatchy
shadows, and there they hid: and after
another long time, what with standing half in
the shade and half out of it, and what with the
slippery-slidy shadows of the trees falling on
them, the Giraffe grew blotchy, and the Zebra

grew stripy, and the Eland and the Koodoo
grew darker, with little wavy grey lines on
their backs like bark on a tree trunk; and so,
though you could hear them and smell them,
you could very seldom see them, and then
only when you knew precisely where to look.
They had a beautiful time in the 'sclusively
speckly-spickly shadows of the forest, while
the Leopard and the Ethiopian ran about over
the 'sclusively greyish-yellowish-reddish High
Veldt outside, wondering where all their
breakfasts and their dinners and their teas
had gone. At last they were so hungry that
they ate rats and beetles and rock-rabbits, the
Leopard and the Ethiopian, and then they had
the Big Tummy-ache, both together; and then
they met Baviaan—the dog-headed, barking
Baboon, who is Quite the Wisest Animal in All
South Africa.

Said Leopard to Baviaan (and it was a very
hot day), 'Where has all the game gone?'

And Baviaan winked. *He* knew.

Said the Ethiopian to Baviaan, 'Can you tell
me the present habitat of the aboriginal
Fauna?' (That meant just the same thing, but
the Ethiopian always used long words. He
was a grown-up.)

And Baviaan winked. *He* knew.

Then said Baviaan, 'The game has gone into

other spots; and my advice to you, Leopard, is to go into other spots as soon as you can.'

And the Ethiopian said, 'That is all very fine, but I wish to know whither the aboriginal Fauna has migrated.'

Then said Baviaan, 'The aboriginal Fauna has joined the aboriginal Flora because it was high time for a change; and my advice to you, Ethiopian, is to change as soon as you can.'

That puzzled the Leopard and the Ethiopian, but they set off to look for the aboriginal Flora, and presently, after ever so many days, they saw a great, high, tall forest full of tree trunks all 'sclusively speckled and sprottled and spottled, dotted and splashed and slashed and hatched and cross-hatched with shadows. (Say that quickly aloud, and you will see how *very* shadowy the forest must have been.)

'What is this,' said the Leopard, 'that is so 'sclusively dark, and yet so full of little pieces of light?'

'I don't know,' said the Ethiopian, 'but it ought to be the aboriginal Flora. I can smell Giraffe, and I can hear Giraffe, but I can't see Giraffe.'

'That's curious,' said the Leopard. 'I suppose it is because we have just come in out of the sunshine. I can smell Zebra, and I can hear Zebra, but I can't see Zebra.'

'Wait a bit,' said the Ethiopian. 'It's a long time since we've hunted 'em. Perhaps we've forgotten what they were like.'

'Fiddle!' said the Leopard. 'I remember them perfectly on the High Veldt, especially their marrow-bones. Giraffe is about seventeen feet high, of a 'sclusively fulvous golden-yellow from head to heel; and Zebra is about four and a half feet high, of a 'sclusively grey-fawn colour from head to heel.'

'Umm,' said the Ethiopian, looking into the speckly-spickly shadows of the aboriginal Flora-forest. 'Then they ought to show up in this dark place like ripe bananas in a smoke-house.'

But they didn't. The Leopard and the Ethiopian hunted all day; and though they could smell them and hear them, they never saw one of them.

'For goodness' sake,' said the Leopard at tea-time, 'let us wait till it gets dark. This daylight hunting is a perfect scandal.'

So they waited till dark, and then the Leopard heard something breathing sniffily in the starlight that fell all stripy through the branches, and he jumped at the noise, and it smelt like Zebra, and it felt like Zebra, and when he knocked it down it kicked like Zebra, but he couldn't see it. So he said, 'Be quiet, O you person without any form. I am going to sit on your head till morning, because there is something about you that I don't understand.'

Presently he heard a grunt and a crash and a scramble, and the Ethiopian called out, 'I've caught a thing that I can't see. It smells like Giraffe, and it kicks like Giraffe, but it hasn't any form.'

'Don't you trust it,' said the Leopard. 'Sit on its head till the morning—same as me. They haven't any form—any of 'em.'

So they sat down on them hard till bright morning-time, and then Leopard said, 'What have you at your end of the table, Brother?'

The Ethiopian scratched his head and said, 'It ought to be 'sclusively a rich fulvous orange-tawny from head to heel, and it ought to be Giraffe; but it is covered all over with chestnut blotches. What have you at *your* end of the table, Brother?'

And the Leopard scratched his head and said, 'It ought to be 'sclusively a delicate greyish-fawn, and it ought to be Zebra; but it is covered all over with black and purple stripes. What in the world have you been doing to yourself, Zebra? Don't you know that if you were on the High Veldt I could see you ten miles off? You haven't any form.'

'Yes,' said the Zebra, 'but this isn't the High Veldt. Can't you see?'

'I can now,' said the Leopard. 'But I couldn't all yesterday. How is it done?'

'Let us up,' said the Zebra, 'and we will show you.'

They let the Zebra and the Giraffe get up; and Zebra moved away to some little thorn-bushes where the sunlight fell all stripy, and Giraffe moved off to some tallish trees where the shadows fell all blotchy.

'Now watch,' said the Zebra and the Giraffe. 'This is the way it's done. One—two—three! And where's your breakfast?'

Leopard stared, and Ethiopian stared, but all they could see were stripy shadows and blotched shadows in the forest, but never a sign of Zebra and Giraffe. They had just walked off and hidden themselves in the shadowy forest.

'Hi! Hi!' said the Ethiopian. 'That's a trick worth learning. Take a lesson by it, Leopard. You show up in this dark place like a bar of soap in a coal-scuttle.'

'Ho! Ho!' said the Leopard. 'Would it surprise you very much to know that you show up in this dark place like a mustard-plaster on a sack of coals?'

'Well, calling names won't catch dinner,'

said the Ethiopian. 'The long and the little of it is that we don't match our backgrounds. I'm going to take Baviaan's advice. He told me I ought to change; and as I've nothing to change except my skin I'm going to change that.'

'What to?' said the Leopard, tremendously excited.

'To a nice working blackish-brownish colour, with a little purple in it, and touches of slaty-blue. It will be the very thing for hiding in hollows and behind trees.'

So he changed his skin then and there, and the Leopard was more excited than ever; he had never seen a man change his skin before.

'But what about me?' he said, when the Ethiopian had worked his last little finger into his fine new black skin.

'You take Baviaan's advice too. He told you to go into spots.'

'So I did,' said the Leopard. 'I went into other spots as fast as I could. I went into this spot with you, and a lot of good it has done me.'

'Oh,' said the Ethiopian, 'Baviaan didn't mean spots in South Africa. He meant spots on your skin.'

'What's the use of that?' said the Leopard.

'Think of Giraffe,' said the Ethiopian. 'Or if you prefer stripes, think of Zebra. They find

their spots and stripes give them per-fect sat-
isfaction.'

'Umm,' said the Leopard. 'I wouldn't look
like Zebra—not for ever so.'

'Well, make up your mind,' said the Ethiopian, 'because I'd hate to go hunting without
you, but I must if you insist on looking like a
sun-flower against a tarred fence.'

'I'll take spots, then,' said the Leopard; 'but
don't make 'em too vulgar-big. I wouldn't look
like Giraffe—not for ever so.'

'I'll make 'em with the tips of my fingers,'
said the Ethiopian. 'There's plenty of black
left on my skin still. Stand over!'

Then the Ethiopian put his five fingers close
together (there was plenty of black left on his
new skin still) and pressed them all over the
Leopard, and wherever the five fingers
touched they left five little black marks, all
close together. You can see them on any Leopard's skin you like, Best Beloved. Sometimes
the fingers slipped and the marks got a little
blurred; but if you look closely at any Leopard
now you will see that there are always five
spots—off five fat black finger-tips.

'Now you *are* a beauty!' said the Ethiopian.
'You can lie out on the bare ground and look
like a heap of pebbles. You can lie out on the
naked rocks and look like a piece of pudding-

'Now you *are* a beauty!' said the Ethiopian.

stone. You can lie out on a leafy branch and look like sunshine sifting through the leaves; and you can lie right across the centre of a path and look like nothing in particular. Think of that and purr!'

'But if I'm all this,' said the Leopard, 'why didn't you go spotty too?'

'Oh, plain black's best for me,' said the Ethiopian. 'Now come along and we'll see if we can't get even with Mr. One-Two-Three-Where's-your-Breakfast!'

So they went away and lived happily ever afterward, Best Beloved. That is all.

Oh, now and then you will hear grown-ups say, 'Can the Ethiopian change his skin or the Leopard his spots?' I don't think even grown-ups would keep on saying such a silly thing if the Leopard and the Ethiopian hadn't done it once—do you? But they will never do it again, Best Beloved. They are quite contented as they are.

I AM the Most Wise Baviaan, saying in
    most wise tones,
'Let us melt into the landscape—just us
    two by our lones.'
People have come—in a carriage—
    calling. But Mummy is there. . . .
Yes, I can go if you take me—Nurse says
    she don't care.
Let's go up to the pig-sties and sit on the
    farmyard rails!
Let's say things to the bunnies, and
    watch 'em skitter their tails!
Let's—oh, *anything*, daddy, so long as
    it's you and me,
And going truly exploring, and not being
    in till tea!
Here's your boots (I've brought 'em),
    and here's your cap and stick,
And here's your pipe and tobacco. Oh,
    come along out of it—quick!

The Crab That Played
with the Sea

BEFORE THE HIGH and Far-Off Times, O my Best Beloved, came the Time of the Very Beginnings; and that was in the days when the Eldest Magician was getting Things ready. First he got the Earth ready; then he got the Sea ready; and then he told all the Animals that they could come out and play. And the Animals said, 'O Eldest Magician, what shall we play at?' and he said, 'I will show you.' He took the Elephant—All-the-Elephant-there-was—and said, 'Play at being an Elephant,' and All-the-Elephant-there-was played. He took the Beaver—All-the-Beaver-there-was—and said, 'Play at being a Beaver,' and All-the-Beaver-there-was played. He took the Cow—All-the-Cow-there-was—and said, 'Play at being a Cow,' and All-the-Cow-there-was played. He took the Turtle—All-the-Turtle-there-was—and said, 'Play at being a Turtle,' and All-the-Turtle-there-was played. One by one he took all the beasts and birds and fishes and told them what to play at.

But towards evening, when people and things grow restless and tired, there came up the Man (With his own little girl-daughter?)—Yes, with his own best-beloved little girl-daughter sitting upon his shoulder, and he said, 'What is this play, Eldest Magician?' And the Eldest Magician said, 'Ho, Son of Adam, this is the play of the Very Beginning; but you are too wise for this play.' And the Man saluted and said, 'Yes, I am too wise for this play; but see that you make all the Animals obedient to me.'

Now, while the two were talking together, Pau Amma the Crab, who was next in the game, scuttled off sideways and stepped into the sea, saying to himself, 'I will play my play alone in the deep waters, and I will never be obedient to this son of Adam.' Nobody saw him go away except the little girl-daughter where she leaned on the Man's shoulder. And the play went on till there were no more Animals left without orders; and the Eldest Magician wiped the fine dust off his hands and walked about the world to see how the Animals were playing.

He went North, Best Beloved, and he found

All-the-Elephant-there-was digging with his tusks and stamping with his feet in the nice new clean earth that had been made ready for him.

'*Kun?*' said All-the-Elephant-there-was, meaning, 'Is this right?'

'*Payah kun,*' said the Eldest Magician, meaning, 'That is quite right'; and he breathed upon the great rocks and lumps of earth that All-the-Elephant-there-was had thrown up, and they became the great Himalayan Mountains, and you can look them out on the map.

He went East, and he found All-the-Cow-there-was feeding in the field that had been made ready for her, and she licked her tongue round a whole forest at a time, and swallowed it and sat down to chew her cud.

'*Kun?*' said All-the-Cow-there-was.

'*Payah kun,*' said the Eldest Magician; and he breathed upon the bare patch where she had eaten, and upon the place where she had sat down, and one became the great Indian Desert, and the other became the Desert of Sahara, and you can look them out on the map.

He went West, and he found All-the-Beaver-there-was making a beaver-dam across the mouths of broad rivers that had been got ready for him.

'*Kun?*' said All-the-Beaver-there-was.

'*Payah kun,*' said the Eldest Magician; and he breathed upon the fallen trees and the still water, and they became the Everglades in Florida, and you may look them out on the map.

Then he went South and found All-the-Turtle-there-was scratching with his flippers in the sand that had been got ready for him, and the sand and the rocks whirled through the air and fell far off into the sea.

'*Kun?*' said All-the-Turtle-there-was.

'*Payah kun,*' said the Eldest Magician; and he breathed upon the sand and the rocks, where they had fallen in the sea, and they became the most beautiful islands of Borneo, Celebes, Sumatra, Java, and the rest of the Malay Archipelago, and you can look *them* out on the map!

By and by the Eldest Magician met the Man on the banks of the Perak River, and said, 'Ho! Son of Adam, are all the Animals obedient to you?'

'Yes,' said the Man.

'Is all the Earth obedient to you?'

'Yes,' said the Man.

'Is all the Sea obedient to you?'

'No,' said the Man. 'Once a day and once a night the Sea runs up the Perak River and drives the sweet-water back into the forest, so that my house is made wet; once a day and once a night it runs down the river and draws all the water after it, so that there is nothing left but mud, and my canoe is upset. Is that the play you told it to play?'

'No,' said the Eldest Magician. 'That is a new and a bad play.'

'Look!' said the Man, and as he spoke the great Sea came up the mouth of the Perak River, driving the river backwards till·it over-flowed all the dark forests for miles and miles, and flooded the Man's house.

'This is wrong. Launch your canoe and we will find out who is playing with the Sea,' said the Eldest Magician. They stepped into the canoe; the little girl-daughter came with them; and the Man took his *kris*—a curving, wavy dagger with a blade like a flame,—and they pushed out on the Perak River. Then the Sea began to run back and back, and the canoe was sucked out of the mouth of the Perak River, past Selangor, past Malacca, past Singapore, out and out to the Island of Bintang, as though it had been pulled by a string.

Then the Eldest Magician stood up and shouted, 'Ho! beasts, birds, and fishes, that I took between my hands at the Very Beginning and taught the play that you should play, which one of you is playing with the Sea?'

Then all the beasts, birds, and fishes said together, 'Eldest Magician, we play the plays that you taught us to play—we and our children's children. But not one of us plays with the Sea.'

Then the Moon rose big and full over the water, and the Eldest Magician said to the hunchbacked old man who sits in the Moon spinning a fishing-line with which he hopes one day to catch the world, 'Ho! Fisher of the Moon, are you playing with the Sea?'

'No,' said the Fisherman, 'I am spinning a line with which I shall some day catch the world; but I do not play with the Sea.' And he went on spinning his line.

Now there is also a Rat up in the Moon who always bites the old Fisherman's line as fast as it is made, and the Eldest Magician said to him, 'Ho! Rat of the Moon, are *you* playing with the Sea?'

And the Rat said, 'I am too busy biting through the line that this old Fisherman is spinning. I do not play with the Sea.' And he went on biting the line.

Then the little girl-daughter put up her little soft brown arms with the beautiful white shell bracelets and said, 'O Eldest Magician! when my father here talked to you at the Very Beginning, and I leaned upon his shoulder while the beasts were being taught their plays, one beast went away naughtily into the Sea before you had taught him his play.'

And the Eldest Magician said, 'How wise are little children who see and are silent! What was that beast like?'

And the little girl-daughter said, 'He was round and he was flat; and his eyes grew upon stalks; and he walked sideways like this; and he was covered with strong armour upon his back.'

And the Eldest Magician said, 'How wise are little children who speak truth! Now I know where Pau Amma went. Give me the paddle!'

So he took the paddle; but there was no need to paddle, for the water flowed steadily past all the islands till they came to the place called Pusat Tasek—the Heart of the Sea— where the great hollow is that leads down to the heart of the world, and in that hollow grows the Wonderful Tree, Pauh Janggi, that bears the magic twin-nuts. Then the Eldest Magician slid his arm up to the shoulder through the deep warm water, and under the roots of the Wonderful Tree he touched the broad back of Pau Amma the Crab. And Pau

Amma settled down at the touch, and all the
Sea rose up as water rises in a basin when
you put your hand into it.

'Ah!' said the Eldest Magician. 'Now I know
who has been playing with the Sea'; and he
called out, 'What are you doing, Pau Amma?'

And Pau Amma, deep down below, an-
swered, 'Once a day and once a night I go out
to look for my food. Once a day and once a
night I return. Leave me alone.'

Then the Eldest Magician said, 'Listen, Pau
Amma. When you go out from your cave the
waters of the Sea pour down into Pusat
Tasek, and all the beaches of all the islands
are left bare, and the little fish die, and Raja
Moyang Kaban, the King of the Elephants, his
legs are made muddy. When you come back
and sit in Pusat Tasek, the waters of the Sea
rise, and half the little islands are drowned,
and the Man's house is flooded, and Raja
Abdullah, the King of the Crocodiles, his
mouth is filled with the salt water.'

Then Pau Amma, deep down below, laughed
and said, 'I did not know I was so important.
Henceforward I will go out seven times a day,
and the waters shall never be still.'

And the Eldest Magician said, 'I cannot
make you play the play you were meant to
play, Pau Amma, because you escaped me at

the Very Beginning; but if you are not afraid, come up and we will talk about it.'

'I am not afraid,' said Pau Amma, and he rose to the top of the sea in the moonlight. There was nobody in the world so big as Pau Amma—for he was the King Crab of all Crabs. Not a common Crab, but a King Crab. One side of his great shell touched the beach at Sarawak; the other touched the beach at Pahang; and he was taller than the smoke of three volcanoes! As he rose up through the branches of the Wonderful Tree he tore off one of the great twin-fruits—the magic double-kernelled nuts that make people young,—and the little girl-daughter saw it bobbing alongside the canoe, and pulled it in and began to pick out the soft eyes of it with her little golden scissors.

'Now,' said the Magician, 'make a Magic, Pau Amma, to show that you are really important.'

Pau Amma rolled his eyes and waved his legs, but he could only stir up the Sea, because, though he was a King Crab, he was nothing more than a Crab, and the Eldest Magician laughed.

'You are not so important after all, Pau Amma,' he said. 'Now, let me try,' and he made a Magic with his left hand—with just the little

He rose to the top of the sea in the moonlight.

finger of his left hand—and—lo and behold, Best Beloved, Pau Amma's hard, blue-green-black shell fell off him as a husk falls off a cocoa-nut, and Pau Amma was left all soft—soft as the little crabs that you sometimes find on the beach, Best Beloved.

'Indeed, you are very important,' said the Eldest Magician. 'Shall I ask the Man here to cut you with his *kris*? Shall I send for Raja Moyang Kaban, the King of the Elephants, to pierce you with his tusks? or shall I call Raja Abdullah, the King of the Crocodiles, to bite you?'

And Pau Amma said, 'I am ashamed! Give me back my hard shell and let me go back to Pusat Tasek, and I will only stir out once a day and once a night to get my food.'

And the Eldest Magician said, 'No, Pau Amma, I will *not* give you back your shell, for you will grow bigger and prouder and stronger, and perhaps you will forget your promise, and you will play with the Sea once more.'

Then Pau Amma said, 'What shall I do? I am so big that I can only hide in Pusat Tasek, and if I go anywhere else, all soft as I am now, the sharks and the dogfish will eat me. And if I go to Pusat Tasek, all soft as I am now, though I may be safe, I can never stir out to get my food, and so I shall die.' Then he waved his legs and lamented.

'Listen, Pau Amma,' said the Eldest Magician. 'I cannot make you play the play you were meant to play, because you escaped me at the Very Beginning; but if you choose, I can make every stone and every hole and every bunch of weed in all the seas a safe Pusat Tasek for you and your children for always.'

Then Pau Amma said, 'That is good, but I do not choose yet. Look! there is that Man who talked to you at the Very Beginning. If he had not taken up your attention I should not have grown tired of waiting and run away, and all this would never have happened. What will *he* do for me?'

And the Man said, 'If you choose, I will make a Magic, so that both the deep water and the dry ground will be a home for you and your children—so that you shall be able to hide both on the land and in the sea.'

And Pau Amma said, 'I do not choose yet. Look! there is that girl who saw me running away at the Very Beginning. If she had spoken then, the Eldest Magician would have called me back, and all this would never have happened. What will *she* do for me?'

And the little girl-daughter said, 'This is a good nut that I am eating. If you choose, I will

make a Magic and I will give you this pair of
scissors, very sharp and strong, so that you
and your children can eat cocoa-nuts like this
all day long when you come up from the Sea
to the land; or you can dig a Pusat Tasek for
yourself with the scissors that belong to you
when there is no stone or hole near by; and
when the earth is too hard, by the help of
these same scissors you can run up a tree.'

And Pau Amma said, 'I do not choose yet,
for, all soft as I am, these gifts would not help
me. Give me back my shell, O Eldest Magician, and then I will play your play.'

And the Eldest Magician said, 'I will give it
back, Pau Amma, for eleven months of the
year; but on the twelfth month of every year it
shall grow soft again, to remind you and all
your children that I can make magics, and to
keep you humble, Pau Amma; for I see that if
you can run both under the water and on land,
you will grow too bold; and if you can climb
trees and crack nuts and dig holes with your
scissors, you will grow too greedy, Pau
Amma.'

Then Pau Amma thought a little and said, 'I
have made my choice. I will take all the gifts.'

Then the Eldest Magician made a Magic
with the right hand, with all five fingers of his
right hand, and lo and behold, Best Beloved,

Pau Amma grew smaller and smaller and smaller, till at last there was only a little green crab swimming in the water alongside the canoe, crying in a very small voice, 'Give me the scissors!'

And the girl-daughter picked him up on the palm of her little brown hand, and sat him in the bottom of the canoe and gave him her scissors, and he waved them in his little arms, and opened them and shut them and snapped them, and said, 'I can eat nuts. I can crack shells. I can dig holes. I can climb trees. I can breathe in the dry air, and I can find a safe Pusat Tasek under every stone. I did not know I was so important. *Kun?*' (Is this right?)

'*Payah kun,*' said the Eldest Magician, and he laughed and gave him his blessing; and little Pau Amma scuttled over the side of the canoe into the water; and he was so tiny that he could have hidden under the shadow of a dry leaf on land or of a dead shell at the bottom of the sea.

'Was that well done?' said the Eldest Magician.

'Yes,' said the Man. 'But now we must go back to Perak, and that is a weary way to paddle. If we had waited till Pau Amma had gone out of Pusat Tasek and come home, the water would have carried us there by itself.'

'You are lazy,' said the Eldest Magician. 'So your children shall be lazy. They shall be the laziest people in the world. They shall be called the Malazy—the lazy people'; and he held up his finger to the Moon and said, 'O Fisherman, here is this Man too lazy to row home. Pull his canoe home with your line, Fisherman.'

'No,' said the Man. 'If I am to be lazy all my days, let the Sea work for me twice a day for ever. That will save paddling.'

And the Eldest Magician laughed and said, '*Payah kun*' (That is right).

And the Rat of the Moon stopped biting the line; and the Fisherman let his line down till it touched the Sea, and he pulled the whole deep Sea along, past the Island of Bintang, past Singapore, past Malacca, past Selangor, till the canoe whirled into the mouth of the Perak River again.

'*Kun?*' said the Fisherman of the Moon.

'*Payah kun,*' said the Eldest Magician. 'See now that you pull the Sea twice a day and twice a night for ever, so that the Malazy fishermen may be saved paddling. But be careful not to do it too hard, or I shall make a Magic on you as I did to Pau Amma.'

Then they all went up the Perak River and went to bed, Best Beloved.

Now listen and attend!

From that day to this the Moon has always pulled the Sea up and down and made what we call the tides. Sometimes the Fisher of the Sea pulls a little too hard, and then we get spring-tides; and sometimes he pulls a little too softly, and then we get what are called neap-tides; but nearly always he is careful, because of the Eldest Magician.

And Pau Amma? You can see when you go to the beach, how all Pau Amma's babies make little Pusat Taseks for themselves under every stone and bunch of weed on the sands; you can see them waving their little scissors; and in some parts of the world they truly live on the dry land and run up the palm-trees and eat cocoa-nuts, exactly as the girl-daughter promised. But once a year all Pau Ammas must shake off their hard armour and be soft—to remind them of what the Eldest Magician could do. And so it isn't fair to kill or hunt Pau Amma's babies just because old Pau Amma was stupidly rude a very long time ago.

Oh yes! And Pau Amma's babies hate being taken out of their little Pusat Taseks and brought home in pickle-bottles. That is why they nip you with their scissors, and it serves you right!

CHINA-GOING P. and O.'s
Pass Pau Amma's playground close,
And his Pusat Tasek lies
Near the track of most B.I.'s.
N.Y.K. and N.D.L.
Know Pau Amma's home as well
As the Fisher of the Sea knows
'Bens,' M.M.'s, and Rubattinos.
But (and this is rather queer)
A.T.L.'s can *not* come here;
O. and O. and D.O.A.
Must go round another way.
Orient, Anchor, Bibby, Hall,
Never go that way at all.
U.C.S. would have a fit
If it found itself on it.
And if 'Beavers' took their cargoes
To Penang instead of Lagos,
Or a fat Shaw-Savill bore
Passengers to Singapore,
Or a White Star were to try a
Little trip to Sourabaya,
Or a B.S.A. went on
Past Natal to Cheribon,
Then great Mr. Lloyds would come
With a wire and drag them home!

You'll know what my riddle means
When you've eaten mangosteens.

Or if you can't wait till then, ask them to let you

have the outside page of the *Times;* turn over to page 2, where it is marked 'Shipping' on the top left hand; then take the Atlas (and that is the finest picture-book in the world) and see how the names of the places that the steamers go to fit into the names of the places on the map. Any steamer-kiddy ought to be able to do that; but if you can't read, ask some one to show it you.

The Cat That Walked
by Himself

HEAR AND ATTEND and listen; for this befell and behappened and became and was, O my Best Beloved, when the Tame animals were wild. The Dog was wild, and the Horse was wild, and the Cow was wild, and the Sheep was wild, and the Pig was wild—as wild as wild could be—and they walked in the Wet Wild Woods by their wild lones. But the wildest of all the wild animals was the Cat. He walked by himself, and all places were alike to him.

Of course the Man was wild too. He was dreadfully wild. He didn't even begin to be tame till he met the Woman, and she told him that she did not like living in his wild ways. She picked out a nice dry Cave, instead of a heap of wet leaves, to lie down in; and she strewed clean sand on the floor; and she lit a nice fire of wood at the back of the Cave; and she hung a dried wild-horse skin, tail-down, across the opening of the Cave; and she said, 'Wipe your feet, dear, when you come in, and now we'll keep house.'

That night, Best Beloved, they ate wild sheep roasted on the hot stones, and flavoured with wild garlic and wild pepper; and wild duck stuffed with wild rice and wild fenugreek and wild coriander; and marrow-bones of wild oxen; and wild cherries, and wild grenadillas. Then the Man went to sleep in front of the fire ever so happy; but the Woman sat up, combing her hair. She took the bone of the shoulder of mutton—the big flat blade-bone—and she looked at the wonderful marks on it, and she threw more wood on the fire, and she made a Magic. She made the First Singing Magic in the world.

Out in the Wet Wild Woods all the wild animals gathered together where they could see the light of the fire a long way off, and they wondered what it meant.

Then Wild Horse stamped with his wild foot and said, 'O my Friends and O my Enemies, why have the Man and the Woman made that great light in that great Cave, and what harm will it do us?'

Wild Dog lifted up his wild nose and

smelled the smell of the roast mutton, and said, 'I will go up and see and look, and say; for I think it is good. Cat, come with me.'

'Nenni!' said the Cat. 'I am the Cat who walks by himself, and all places are alike to me. I will not come.'

'Then we can never be friends again,' said Wild Dog, and he trotted off to the Cave. But when he had gone a little way the Cat said to himself, 'All places are alike to me. Why should I not go too and see and look and come away at my own liking?' So he slipped after Wild Dog softly, very softly, and hid himself where he could hear everything.

When Wild Dog reached the mouth of the Cave he lifted up the dried horse-skin with his nose and sniffed the beautiful smell of the roast mutton, and the Woman, looking at the blade-bone, heard him, and laughed, and said, 'Here comes the first. Wild Thing out of the Wild Woods, what do you want?'

Wild Dog said, 'O my Enemy and Wife of my Enemy, what is this that smells so good in the Wild Woods?'

Then the Woman picked up a roasted mutton-bone and threw it to Wild Dog, and said, 'Wild Thing out of the Wild Woods, taste and try.' Wild Dog gnawed the bone, and it was more delicious than anything he had ever tasted, and he said, 'O my Enemy and Wife of my Enemy, give me another.'

The Woman said, 'Wild Thing out of the Wild Woods, help my Man to hunt through the day and guard this Cave at night, and I will give you as many roast bones as you need.'

'Ah!' said the Cat, listening. 'This is a very wise Woman, but she is not so wise as I am.'

Wild Dog crawled into the Cave and laid his head on the Woman's lap, and said, 'O my Friend and Wife of my Friend, I will help your Man to hunt through the day, and at night I will guard your Cave.'

'Ah!' said the Cat, listening. 'That is a very foolish Dog.' And he went back through the Wet Wild Woods waving his wild tail, and walking by his wild lone. But he never told anybody.

When the Man waked up he said, 'What is Wild Dog doing here?' And the Woman said, 'His name is not Wild Dog any more, but the First Friend, because he will be our friend for always and always and always. Take him with you when you go hunting.'

Next night the Woman cut great green armfuls of fresh grass from the water-meadows, and dried it before the fire, so that it smelt like new-mown hay, and she sat at the mouth of the Cave and plaited a halter out of horse-hide, and she looked at the shoulder-of-mutton bone—at the big broad blade-bone—and she made a Magic. She made the Second Singing Magic in the world.

Out in the Wild Woods all the wild animals wondered what had happened to Wild Dog, and at last Wild Horse stamped with his foot and said, 'I will go and see and say why Wild Dog has not returned. Cat, come with me.'

'Nenni!' said the Cat. 'I am the Cat who walks by himself, and all places are alike to me. I will not come.' But all the same he followed Wild Horse softly, very softly, and hid himself where he could hear everything.

When the Woman heard Wild Horse tripping and stumbling on his long mane, she laughed and said, 'Here comes the second. Wild Thing out of the Wild Woods, what do you want?'

Wild Horse said, 'O my Enemy and Wife of my Enemy, where is Wild Dog?'

The Woman laughed, and picked up the blade-bone and looked at it, and said, 'Wild Thing out of the Wild Woods, you did not come here for Wild Dog, but for the sake of this good grass.'

And Wild Horse, tripping and stumbling on his long mane, said, 'That is true; give it me to eat.'

The Woman said, 'Wild Thing out of the Wild Woods, bend your wild head and wear what I give you, and you shall eat the wonderful grass three times a day.'

'Ah,' said the Cat, listening, 'this is a clever Woman, but she is not so clever as I am.'

Wild Horse bent his wild head, and the Woman slipped the plaited hide halter over it, and Wild Horse breathed on the Woman's feet and said, 'O my Mistress, and Wife of my Master, I will be your servant for the sake of the wonderful grass.'

'Ah,' said the Cat, listening, 'that is a very foolish Horse.' And he went back through the Wet Wild Woods, waving his wild tail and walking by his wild lone. But he never told anybody.

When the Man and the Dog came back from hunting, the Man said, 'What is Wild Horse doing here?' And the Woman said, 'His name is not Wild Horse any more, but the First Servant, because he will carry us from place to place for always and always and always. Ride on his back when you go hunting.'

Next day, holding her wild head high that her wild horns should not catch in the wild trees, Wild Cow came up to the Cave, and the Cat followed, and hid himself just the same as before; and everything happened just the same as before; and the Cat said the same things as before; and when Wild Cow had promised to give her milk to the Woman every day in exchange for the wonderful grass, the Cat went back through the Wet Wild Woods waving his wild tail and walking by his wild lone, just the same as before. But he never told anybody. And when the Man and the Horse and the Dog came home from hunting and asked the same questions same as before, the Woman said, 'Her name is not Wild Cow any more, but the Giver of Good Food. She will give us the warm white milk for always and always and always, and I will take care of her while you and the First Friend and the First Servant go hunting.'

Next day the Cat waited to see if any other Wild Thing would go up to the Cave, but no one moved in the Wet Wild Woods, so the Cat walked there by himself; and he saw the Woman milking the Cow, and he saw the light of the fire in the Cave, and he smelt the smell of the warm white milk.

Cat said, 'O my Enemy and Wife of my Enemy, where did Wild Cow go?'

The Woman laughed and said, 'Wild Thing out of the Wild Woods, go back to the Woods again, for I have braided up my hair, and I have put away the magic blade-bone, and we have no more need of either friends or servants in our Cave.'

Cat said, 'I am not a friend, and I am not a servant. I am the Cat who walks by himself, and I wish to come into your Cave.'

Woman said, 'Then why did you not come with First Friend on the first night?'

Cat grew very angry and said, 'Has Wild Dog told tales of me?'

Then the Woman laughed and said, 'You are the Cat who walks by himself, and all places are alike to you. You are neither a friend nor a servant. You have said it yourself. Go away and walk by yourself in all places alike.'

Then Cat pretended to be sorry and said, 'Must I never come into the Cave? Must I never sit by the warm fire? Must I never drink the warm white milk? You are very wise and very beautiful. You should not be cruel even to a Cat.'

Woman said, 'I knew I was wise, but I did not know I was beautiful. So I will make a bargain with you. If ever I say one word in your praise, you may come into the Cave.'

'And if you say two words in my praise?' said the Cat.

'I never shall,' said the Woman, 'but if I say two words in your praise, you may sit by the fire in the Cave.'

'And if you say three words?' said the Cat.

'I never shall,' said the Woman, 'but if I say three words in your praise, you may drink the warm white milk three times a day for always and always and always.'

Then the Cat arched his back and said, 'Now let the Curtain at the mouth of the Cave, and the Fire at the back of the Cave, and the Milk-pots that stand beside the Fire, remember what my Enemy and the Wife of my Enemy has said.' And he went away through the Wet Wild Woods waving his wild tail and walking by his wild lone.

That night when the Man and the Horse and the Dog came home from hunting, the Woman did not tell them of the bargain that she had made with the Cat, because she was afraid that they might not like it.

Cat went far and far away and hid himself in the Wet Wild Woods by his wild lone for a long time till the Woman forgot all about him. Only the Bat—the little upside-down Bat— that hung inside the Cave knew where Cat hid; and every evening Bat would fly to Cat with news of what was happening.

One evening Bat said, 'There is a Baby in the Cave. He is new and pink and fat and small, and the Woman is very fond of him.'

'Ah,' said the Cat, listening, 'but what is the Baby fond of?'

'He is fond of things that are soft and

tickle,' said the Bat. 'He is fond of warm things to hold in his arms when he goes to sleep. He is fond of being played with. He is fond of all those things.'

'Ah,' said the Cat, listening, 'then my time has come.'

Next night Cat walked through the Wet Wild Woods and hid very near the Cave till morning-time, and Man and Dog and Horse went hunting. The Woman was busy cooking that morning, and the Baby cried and interrupted. So she carried him outside the Cave and gave him a handful of pebbles to play with. But still the Baby cried.

Then the Cat put out his paddy paw and patted the Baby on the cheek, and it cooed; and the Cat rubbed against its fat knees and tickled it under its fat chin with his tail. And the Baby laughed; and the Woman heard him and smiled.

Then the Bat—the little upside-down Bat— that hung in the mouth of the Cave said, 'O my Hostess and Wife of my Host and Mother of my Host's Son, a Wild Thing from the Wild Woods is most beautifully playing with your Baby.'

'A blessing on that Wild Thing whoever he may be,' said the Woman, straightening her back, 'for I was a busy woman this morning and he has done me a service.'

That very minute and second, Best Beloved, the dried horse-skin Curtain that was stretched tail-down at the mouth of the Cave fell down—*woosh!*—because it remembered the bargain she had made with the Cat; and when the Woman went to pick it up—lo and behold!—the Cat was sitting quite comfy inside the Cave.

'O my Enemy and Wife of my Enemy and Mother of my Enemy,' said the Cat, 'it is I: for you have spoken a word in my praise, and now I can sit within the Cave for always and always and always. But still I am the Cat who walks by himself, and all places are alike to me.'

The Woman was very angry, and shut her lips tight and took up her spinning-wheel and began to spin.

But the Baby cried because the Cat had gone away, and the Woman could not hush it, for it struggled and kicked and grew black in the face.

'O my Enemy and Wife of my Enemy and Mother of my Enemy,' said the Cat, 'take a strand of the thread that you are spinning and tie it to your spinning-whorl and drag it along the floor, and I will show you a Magic that shall make your Baby laugh as loudly as he is now crying.'

'I will do so,' said the Woman, 'because I am

at my wits' end; but I will not thank you for it.'

She tied the thread to the little clay spindle-whorl and drew it across the floor, and the Cat ran after it and patted it with his paws and rolled head over heels, and tossed it backward over his shoulder and chased it between his hind-legs and pretended to lose it, and pounced down upon it again, till the Baby laughed as loudly as it had been crying, and scrambled after the Cat and frolicked all over the Cave till it grew tired and settled down to sleep with the Cat in its arms.

'Now,' said Cat, 'I will sing the Baby a song that shall keep him asleep for an hour.' And he began to purr, loud and low, low and loud, till the Baby fell fast asleep. The Woman smiled as she looked down upon the two of them, and said, 'That was wonderfully done. No question but you are very clever, O Cat.'

That very minute and second, Best Beloved, the smoke of the Fire at the back of the Cave came down in clouds from the roof—*puff!*—because it remembered the bargain she had made with the Cat; and when it had cleared away—lo and behold!—the Cat was sitting quite comfy close to the fire.

'O my Enemy and Wife of my Enemy and Mother of my Enemy,' said the Cat, 'it is I: for you have spoken a second word in my praise,

The Cat ran after it and patted it with his paws.

and now I can sit by the warm fire at the back of the Cave for always and always and always. But still I am the Cat who walks by himself, and all places are alike to me.'

Then the Woman was very very angry, and let down her hair and put more wood on the fire and brought out the broad blade-bone of the shoulder of mutton and began to make a Magic that should prevent her from saying a third word in praise of the Cat. It was not a Singing Magic, Best Beloved, it was a Still Magic; and by and by the Cave grew so still that a little wee-wee mouse crept out of a corner and ran across the floor.

'O my Enemy and Wife of my Enemy and Mother of my Enemy,' said the Cat, 'is that little mouse part of your Magic?'

'Ouh! Chee! No indeed!' said the Woman, and she dropped the blade-bone and jumped upon the footstool in front of the fire and braided up her hair very quick for fear that the mouse should run up it.

'Ah,' said the Cat, watching, 'then the mouse will do me no harm if I eat it?'

'No,' said the Woman, braiding up her hair, 'eat it quickly and I will be ever grateful to you.'

Cat made one jump and caught the little mouse, and the Woman said, 'A hundred thanks. Even the First Friend is not quick enough to catch little mice as you have done. You must be very wise.'

That very moment and second, O Best Beloved, the Milk-pot that stood by the fire cracked in two pieces—*ffft!*—because it remembered the bargain she had made with the Cat; and when the Woman jumped down from the footstool—lo and behold!—the Cat was lapping up the warm white milk that lay in one of the broken pieces.

'O my Enemy and Wife of my Enemy and Mother of my Enemy,' said the Cat, 'it is I: for you have spoken three words in my praise, and now I can drink the warm white milk three times a day for always and always and always. But *still* I am the Cat who walks by himself, and all places are alike to me.'

Then the Woman laughed and set the Cat a bowl of the warm white milk and said, 'O Cat, you are as clever as a man, but remember that your bargain was not made with the Man or the Dog, and I do not know what they will do when they come home.'

'What is that to me?' said the Cat. 'If I have my place in the Cave by the fire and my warm white milk three times a day I do not care what the Man or the Dog can do.'

That evening when the Man and the Dog

came into the Cave, the Woman told them all
the story of the bargain, while the Cat sat by
the fire and smiled. Then the Man said, 'Yes,
but he has not made a bargain, with *me* or
with all proper Men after me.' Then he took
off his two leather boots and he took up his
little stone axe (that makes three) and he
fetched a piece of wood and a hatchet (that is
five altogether), and he set them out in a row
and he said, 'Now we will make *our* bargain.
If you do not catch mice when you are in the
Cave for always and always and always, I will
throw these five things at you whenever I see
you, and so shall all proper Men do after me.'

'Ah,' said the Woman, listening, 'this is a
very clever Cat, but he is not so clever as my
Man.'

The Cat counted the five things (and they
looked very knobby) and he said, 'I will catch
mice when I am in the Cave for always and
always and always; but *still* I am the Cat who
walks by himself, and all places are alike to
me.'

'Not when I am near,' said the Man. 'If you
had not said that last I would have put all
these things away for always and always and
always; but now I am going to throw my two
boots and my little stone axe (that makes
three) at you whenever I meet you. And so
shall all proper Men do after me!'

Then the Dog said, 'Wait a minute. He has not made a bargain with *me* or with all proper Dogs after me.' And he showed his teeth and said, 'If you are not kind to the Baby while I am in the Cave for always and always and always, I will hunt you till I catch you, and when I catch you I will bite you. And so shall all proper Dogs do after me.'

'Ah,' said the Woman, listening, 'this is a very clever Cat, but he is not so clever as the Dog.'

Cat counted the Dog's teeth (and they looked very pointed) and he said, 'I will be kind to the Baby while I am in the Cave, as long as he does not pull my tail too hard, for always and always and always. But *still* I am the Cat that walks by himself, and all places are alike to me!'

'Not when I am near,' said the Dog. 'If you had not said that last I would have shut my mouth for always and always and always; but *now* I am going to hunt you up a tree whenever I meet you. And so shall all proper Dogs do after me.'

Then the Man threw his two boots and his little stone axe (that makes three) at the Cat, and the Cat ran out of the Cave and the Dog chased him up a tree; and from that day to this, Best Beloved, three proper Men out of five will always throw things at a Cat whenever they meet him, and all proper Dogs will chase him up a tree. But the Cat keeps his side of the bargain too. He will kill mice, and he will be kind to Babies when he is in the house, just as long as they do not pull his tail too hard. But when he has done that, and between times, and when the moon gets up and night comes, he is the Cat that walks by himself, and all places are alike to him. Then he goes out to the Wet Wild Woods or up the Wet Wild Trees or on the Wet Wild Roofs, waving his wild tail and walking by his wild lone.

PUSSY can sit by the fire and sing,
  Pussy can climb a tree,
Or play with a silly old cork and string
  To 'muse herself; not me.
But I like *Binkie* my dog, because
  He knows how to behave;
So, *Binkie's* the same as the First Friend
    was,
  And I am the Man in the Cave.

Pussy will play man-Friday till
  It's time to wet her paw
And make her walk on the window-sill
  (For the footprint Crusoe saw);
Then she fluffles her tail and mews,
  And scratches and won't attend.
But *Binkie* will play whatever I choose,
  And he is my true First Friend.

Pussy will rub my knees with her head
  Pretending she loves me hard;
But the very minute I go to my bed
  Pussy runs out in the yard,
And there she stays till the morning-light;
  So I know it is only pretend;
But *Binkie*, he snores at my feet all night,
  And he is my Firstest Friend!

The Butterfly
That Stamped

THIS, O MY BEST BELOVED, is a story—a new and a wonderful story—a story quite different from the other stories—a story about The Most Wise Sovereign Suleiman-bin-Daoud—Solomon the Son of David.

There are three hundred and fifty-five stories about Suleiman-bin-Daoud; but this is not one of them. It is not the story of the Lapwing who found the Water; or the Hoopoe who shaded Suleiman-bin-Daoud from the heat. It is not the story of the Glass Pavement, or the Ruby with the Crooked Hole, or the Gold Bars of Balkis. It is the story of the Butterfly that Stamped.

Now attend all over again and listen!

Suleiman-bin-Daoud was wise. He understood what the beasts said, what the birds said, what the fishes said, and what the insects said. He understood what the rocks said deep under the earth when they bowed in towards each other and groaned; and he understood what the trees said when they rustled in the middle of the morning. He understood everything, from the bishop on the bench to the hyssop on the wall; and Balkis, his Head Queen, the Most Beautiful Queen Balkis, was nearly as wise as he was.

Suleiman-bin-Daoud was strong. Upon the third finger of his right hand he wore a ring. When he turned it once, Afrits and Djinns came out of the earth to do whatever he told them. When he turned it twice, Fairies came down from the sky to do whatever he told them; and when he turned it three times, the very great angel Azrael of the Sword came dressed as a water-carrier, and told him the news of the three worlds,—Above—Below—and Here.

And yet Suleiman-bin-Daoud was not proud. He very seldom showed off, and when he did he was sorry for it. Once he tried to feed all the animals in all the world in one day, but when the food was ready an Animal came out of the deep sea and ate it up in three mouthfuls. Suleiman-bin-Daoud was very surprised and said, 'O Animal, who are you?' And the Animal said, 'O King, live for ever! I am the smallest of thirty thousand brothers, and our home is at the bottom of the sea. We heard that you were going to feed all the animals in all the world, and my brothers sent me to ask when dinner would be ready.' Suleiman-bin-Daoud was more surprised than ever and said, 'O Animal, you have eaten all the dinner that I made ready for all the animals in the world.' And the Animal said, 'O King, live for ever, but do you really call *that* a dinner? Where I come from we each eat twice as much as that between meals.' Then Suleiman-bin-Daoud fell flat on his face and said, 'O Animal! I gave that dinner to show what a great and rich king I was, and not because I really wanted to be kind to the animals. Now I am ashamed, and it serves me right.' Suleiman-bin-Daoud was a really truly wise man, Best Beloved. After that he never forgot that it was silly to show off; and now the real story part of my story begins.

He married ever so many wives. He married nine hundred and ninety-nine wives, besides the Most Beautiful Balkis; and they all lived in a great golden palace in the middle of a lovely garden with fountains. He didn't really want nine hundred and ninety-nine wives, but in those days everybody married ever so many wives, and of course the King had to marry ever so many more just to show that he was the King.

Some of the wives were nice, but some were simply horrid, and the horrid ones quarrelled with the nice ones and made them horrid too, and then they would all quarrel with Suleiman-bin-Daoud, and that was horrid for him. But Balkis the Most Beautiful never quarrelled with Suleiman-bin-Daoud. She loved him too much. She sat in her rooms in the Golden Palace, or walked in the Palace garden, and was truly sorry for him.

Of course if he had chosen to turn his ring on his finger and call up the Djinns and the Afrits they would have magicked all those nine hundred and ninety-nine quarrelsome wives into white mules of the desert or greyhounds or pomegranate seeds; but Suleiman-bin-Daoud thought that that would be showing off. So, when they quarrelled too much, he only walked by himself in one part of the beautiful Palace gardens and wished he had never been born.

One day, when they had quarrelled for three weeks—all nine hundred and ninety-nine wives together—Suleiman-bin-Daoud went out for peace and quiet as usual; and among the orange-trees he met Balkis the Most Beau-

tiful, very sorrowful because Suleiman-bin-
Daoud was so worried. And she said to him,
'O my Lord and Light of my Eyes, turn the ring
upon your finger and show these Queens of
Egypt and Mesopotamia and Persia and China
that you are the great and terrible King.' But
Suleiman-bin-Daoud shook his head and said,
'O my Lady and Delight of my Life, remember
the Animal that came out of the sea and made
me ashamed before all the animals in all the
world because I showed off. Now, if I showed
off before these Queens of Persia and Egypt
and Abyssinia and China, merely because they
worry me, I might be made even more
ashamed than I have been.'

And Balkis the Most Beautiful said, 'O my
Lord and Treasure of my Soul, what will you
do?'

And Sulciman-bin-Daoud said, 'O my Lady
and Content of my Heart, I shall continue to
endure my fate at the hands of these nine
hundred and ninety-nine Queens who vex me
with their continual quarrelling.'

So he went on between the lilies and the
loquats and the roses and the cannas and the
heavy-scented ginger-plants that grew in the
garden, till he came to the great camphor-tree
of Suleiman-bin-Daoud. But Balkis hid among
the tall irises and the spotted bamboos and

the red lilies behind the camphor-tree, so as to be near her own true love, Suleiman-bin-Daoud.

Presently two Butterflies flew under the tree, quarrelling.

Suleiman-bin-Daoud heard one say to the other, 'I wonder at your presumption in talking like this to me. Don't you know that if I stamped with my foot all Suleiman-bin-Daoud's Palace and this garden here would immediately vanish in a clap of thunder?'

Then Suleiman-bin-Daoud forgot his nine hundred and ninety-nine bothersome wives, and laughed, till the camphor-tree shook, at the Butterfly's boast. And he held out his finger and said, 'Little man, come here.'

The Butterfly was dreadfully frightened, but he managed to fly up to the hand of Suleiman-bin-Daoud, and clung there, fanning himself. Suleiman-bin-Daoud bent his head and whispered very softly, 'Little man, you know that all your stamping wouldn't bend one blade of grass. What made you tell that awful fib to your wife?—for doubtless she is your wife.'

The Butterfly looked at Suleiman-bin-Daoud and saw the most wise King's eyes twinkle like stars on a frosty night, and he picked up his courage with both wings, and he put his head on one side and said, 'O King, live for

Presently two Butterflies flew under the tree, quarrelling.

ever. She *is* my wife; and you know what wives are like.'

Suleiman-bin-Daoud smiled in his beard and said, 'Yes, *I* know, little brother.'

'One must keep them in order somehow,' said the Butterfly, 'and she has been quarrelling with me all the morning. I said that to quiet her.'

And Suleiman-bin-Daoud said, 'May it quiet her. Go back to your wife, little brother, and let me hear what you say.'

Back flew the Butterfly to his wife, who was all of a twitter behind a leaf, and she said, 'He heard you! Suleiman-bin-Daoud himself heard you!'

'Heard me!' said the Butterfly. 'Of course he did. I meant him to hear me.'

'And what did he say? Oh, what did he say?'

'Well,' said the Butterfly, fanning himself most importantly, 'between you and me, my dear—of course I don't blame him, because his Palace must have cost a great deal and the oranges are just ripening,—he asked me not to stamp, and I promised I wouldn't.'

'Gracious!' said his wife, and sat quite quiet; but Suleiman-bin-Daoud laughed till the tears ran down his face at the impudence of the bad little Butterfly.

Balkis the Most Beautiful stood up behind

the tree among the red lilies and smiled to herself, for she had heard all this talk. She thought, 'If I am wise I can yet save my Lord from the persecutions of these quarrelsome Queens,' and she held out her finger and whispered softly to the Butterfly's Wife, 'Little woman, come here.' Up flew the Butterfly's Wife, very frightened, and clung to Balkis's white hand.

Balkis bent her beautiful head down and whispered, 'Little woman, do you believe what your husband has just said?'

The Butterfly's Wife looked at Balkis, and saw the Most Beautiful Queen's eyes shining like deep pools with starlight on them, and she picked up her courage with both wings and said, 'O Queen, be lovely for ever. *You* know what men-folk are like.'

And the Queen Balkis, the Wise Balkis of Sheba, put her hand to her lips to hide a smile and said, 'Little sister, *I* know.'

'They get angry,' said the Butterfly's Wife, fanning herself quickly, 'over nothing at all, but we must humour them, O Queen. They never mean half they say. If it pleases my husband to believe that I believe he can make Suleiman-bin-Daoud's Palace disappear by stamping his foot, I'm sure *I* don't care. He'll forget all about it to-morrow.'

'Little sister,' said Balkis, 'you are quite right; but next time he begins to boast, take him at his word. Ask him to stamp, and see what will happen. *We* know what men-folk are like, don't we? He'll be very much ashamed.'

Away flew the Butterfly's Wife to her husband, and in five minutes they were quarrelling worse than ever.

'Remember!' said the Butterfly. 'Remember what I can do if I stamp my foot.'

'I don't believe you one little bit,' said the Butterfly's Wife. 'I should very much like to see it done. Suppose you stamp now.'

'I promised Suleiman-bin-Daoud that I wouldn't,' said the Butterfly, 'and I don't want to break my promise.'

'It wouldn't matter if you did,' said his wife. 'You couldn't bend a blade of grass with your stamping. I dare you to do it,' she said. 'Stamp! Stamp! Stamp!'

Suleiman-bin-Daoud, sitting under the camphor-tree, heard every word of this, and he laughed as he had never laughed in his life before. He forgot all about his Queens; he forgot about the Animal that came out of the sea; he forgot about showing off. He just laughed with joy, and Balkis, on the other side of the tree, smiled because her own true love was so joyful.

Presently the Butterfly, very hot and puffy, came whirling back under the shadow of the camphor-tree and said to Suleiman, 'She wants me to stamp! She wants to see what will happen, O Suleiman-bin-Daoud! You know I can't do it, and now she'll never believe a word I say. She'll laugh at me to the end of my days!'

'No, little brother,' said Suleiman-bin-Daoud, 'she will never laugh at you again,' and he turned the ring on his finger—just for the little Butterfly's sake, not for the sake of showing off,—and, lo and behold, four huge Djinns came out of the earth!

'Slaves,' said Suleiman-bin-Daoud, 'when this gentleman on my finger' (that was where the impudent Butterfly was sitting) 'stamps his left front forefoot you will make my Palace and these gardens disappear in a clap of thunder. When he stamps again you will bring them back carefully.'

'Now, little brother,' he said, 'go back to your wife and stamp all you've a mind to.'

Away flew the Butterfly to his wife, who was crying, 'I dare you to do it! I dare you to do it! Stamp! Stamp now! Stamp!' Balkis saw the four vast Djinns stoop down to the four corners of the gardens with the Palace in the middle, and she clapped her hands softly and said, 'At last Suleiman-bin-Daoud will do for the sake of a Butterfly what he ought to have done long ago for his own sake, and the quarrelsome Queens will be frightened!'

Then the Butterfly stamped. The Djinns jerked the Palace and the gardens a thousand miles into the air: there was a most awful thunder-clap, and everything grew inky-black. The Butterfly's Wife fluttered about in the dark, crying, 'Oh, I'll be good! I'm so sorry I spoke! Only bring the gardens back, my dear darling husband, and I'll never contradict again.'

The Butterfly was nearly as frightened as his wife, and Suleiman-bin-Daoud laughed so much that it was several minutes before he found breath enough to whisper to the Butterfly, 'Stamp again, little brother. Give me back my Palace, most great magician.'

'Yes, give him back his Palace,' said the Butterfly's Wife, still flying about in the dark like a moth. 'Give him back his Palace, and don't let's have any more horrid magic.'

'Well, my dear,' said the Butterfly as bravely as he could, 'you see what your nagging has led to. Of course it doesn't make any difference to *me*—I'm used to this kind of thing— but as a favour to you and to Suleiman-bin-Daoud I don't mind putting things right.'

So he stamped once more, and that instant
the Djinns let down the Palace and the gardens, without even a bump. The sun shone on
the dark-green orange-leaves; the fountains
played among the pink Egyptian lilies; the
birds went on singing; and the Butterfly's Wife
lay on her side under the camphor-tree wag-
gling her wings and panting, 'Oh, I'll be good!
I'll be good!'

Suleiman-bin-Daoud could hardly speak for
laughing. He leaned back all weak and hic-
coughy, and shook his finger at the Butterfly
and said, 'O great wizard, what is the sense of
returning to me my Palace if at the same time
you slay me with mirth!'

Then came a terrible noise, for all the nine
hundred and ninety-nine Queens ran out of
the Palace shrieking and shouting and calling
for their babies. They hurried down the great
marble steps below the fountain, one hundred
abreast, and the Most Wise Balkis went state-
lily forward to meet them and said, 'What is
your trouble, O Queens?'

They stood on the marble steps one hundred abreast and shouted, '*What* is our trouble? We were living peacefully in our golden
Palace, as is our custom, when upon a sudden
the Palace disappeared, and we were left sitting in a thick and noisome darkness; and it

thundered, and Djinns and Afrits moved about
in the darkness! *That* is our trouble, O Head
Queen, and we are most extremely troubled
on account of that trouble, for it was a trou-
blesome trouble, unlike any trouble we have
known.'

Then Balkis the Most Beautiful Queen—
Suleiman-bin-Daoud's Very Best Beloved—
Queen that was of Sheba and Sabie and the
Rivers of the Gold of the South—from the
Desert of Zinn to the Towers of Zimbabwe—
Balkis, almost as wise as the Most Wise
Suleiman-bin-Daoud himself, said, 'It is noth-
ing, O Queens! A Butterfly has made com-
plaint against his wife because she quarrelled
with him, and it has pleased our Lord
Suleiman-bin-Daoud to teach her a lesson in
low-speaking and humbleness, for that is
counted a virtue among the wives of the
butterflies.'

Then up and spoke an Egyptian Queen—the
daughter of a Pharaoh—and she said, 'Our
Palace cannot be plucked up by the roots like
a leek for the sake of a little insect. No!
Suleiman-bin-Daoud must be dead, and what
we heard and saw was the earth thundering
and darkening at the news.'

Then Balkis beckoned that bold queen without looking at her, and said to her and to the others, 'Come and see.'

They came down the marble steps, one hundred abreast, and beneath his camphor-tree, still weak with laughing, they saw the Most Wise King Suleiman-bin-Daoud rocking back and forth with a Butterfly on either hand, and they heard him say, 'O wife of my brother in the air, remember after this to please your husband in all things, lest he be provoked to stamp his foot yet again; for he has said that he is used to this Magic, and he is most eminently a great magician—one who steals away the very Palace of Suleiman-bin-Daoud himself. Go in peace, little folk!' And he kissed them on the wings, and they flew away.

Then all the Queens except Balkis—the Most Beautiful and Splendid Balkis, who stood apart smiling—fell flat on their faces, for they said, 'If these things are done when a Butterfly is displeased with his wife, what shall be done to us who have vexed our King with our loud-speaking and open quarrelling through many days?'

Then they put their veils over their heads, and they put their hands over their mouths, and they tiptoed back to the Palace most mousy-quiet.

Then Balkis—the Most Beautiful and Excellent Balkis—went forward through the red lilies into the shade of the camphor-tree and laid her hand upon Suleiman-bin-Daoud's shoulder and said, 'O my Lord and Treasure of my Soul, rejoice, for we have taught the Queens of Egypt and Ethiopia and Abyssinia and Persia and India and China with a great and a memorable teaching.'

And Suleiman-bin-Daoud, still looking after the Butterflies where they played in the sunlight, said, 'O my Lady and Jewel of my Felicity, when did this happen? For I have been jesting with a Butterfly ever since I came into the garden.' And he told Balkis what he had done.

Balkis—the Tender and Most Lovely Balkis—said, 'O my Lord and Regent of my Existence, I hid behind the camphor-tree and saw it all. It was I who told the Butterfly's Wife to ask the Butterfly to stamp, because I hoped that for the sake of the jest my Lord would make some great Magic and that the Queens would see it and be frightened.' And she told him what the Queens had said and seen and thought.

Then Suleiman-bin-Daoud rose up from his seat under the camphor-tree, and stretched his arms and rejoiced and said, 'O my Lady and Sweetener of my Days, know that if I had made a Magic against my Queens for the sake of pride or anger, as I made that feast for all the animals, I should certainly have been put to shame. But by means of your wisdom I made the Magic for the sake of a jest and for the sake of a little Butterfly, and—behold—it has also delivered me from the vexations of my vexatious wives! Tell me, therefore, O my Lady and Heart of my Heart, how did you come to be so wise?'

And Balkis the Queen, beautiful and tall, looked up into Suleiman-bin-Daoud's eyes and put her head a little on one side, just like the Butterfly, and said, 'First, O my Lord, because I loved you; and secondly, O my Lord, because I know what women-folk are.'

Then they went up to the Palace and lived happily ever afterwards.

But wasn't it clever of Balkis?

THERE was never a Queen like Balkis,
From here to the wide world's end;
But Balkis talked to a butterfly
As you would talk to a friend.

There was never a King like Solomon,
Not since the world began;
But Solomon talked to a butterfly
As a man would talk to a man.

She was Queen of Sabæa—
And *he* was Asia's Lord—
But they both of 'em talked to butterflies
When they took their walks abroad!